For Michele, Celeste, and Deb—mahalo—and for Rudy, who always comes back to me
—Suz

For Linda, who encouraged many birds to fly
—Scott

## ⇝ Author's Note—Fact Meets Fiction ⇜

In places with mild winters, cattle egrets and cows are a familiar pair and a perfect example of symbiosis—a relationship that benefits both species. Grazing cattle moving through a pasture kick up insects for the egrets to eat. In return, egrets perch on the cows to pick off ticks and catch flies that would otherwise be bothersome.

Text Copyright © 2021 Susan Blackaby
Illustration Copyright © 2021 Scott Brundage
Design Copyright © 2021 Sleeping Bear Press
All rights reserved. No part of this book may be reproduced in any manner without the express written consent of the publisher, except in the case of brief excerpts in critical reviews and articles. All inquiries should be addressed to:

SLEEPING BEAR PRESS™

2395 South Huron Parkway, Suite 200, Ann Arbor, MI 48104
www.sleepingbearpress.com © Sleeping Bear Press
Printed and bound in the United States
10 9 8 7 6 5 4 3 2 1
Library of Congress Cataloging-in-Publication Data
Names: Blackaby, Susan, author. | Brundage, Scott, illustrator.
Title: Where's my cow? / by Susan Blackaby and illustrated by Scott Brundage.
Other titles: Where is my cow?
Description: Ann Arbor, MI : Sleeping Bear Press, [2021] | Audience: Ages 4-8. | Summary: A little egret is afraid to fly to the seashore because he fears he will not find his way back to his best friend, a cow, but she encourages the little egret to explore and looks for ways to encourage him.
Identifiers: LCCN 2021005301 | ISBN 9781534111073 (hardcover)
Subjects: CYAC: Fear–Fiction. | Problem solving–Fiction. | Herons–Fiction. | Cows–Fiction.
Classification: LCC PZ7.B5318 Wh 2021 | DDC [E]–dc23
LC record available at https://lccn.loc.gov/2021005301

# WHERE'S MY COW?

By Susan Blackaby and Illustrated by Scott Brundage

PUBLISHED *by* SLEEPING BEAR PRESS™

In a pasture near the sea,
a flock of egrets lived with a herd of cows.
Each morning, when the birds whirled off to
explore the shore, one little egret stayed behind.

The flock squawked and screeched,
catching the beachy breeze.
"C'mon! C'mon!"

But the little egret wouldn't budge.
So much hubbub made him woozy.
And the beach seemed so far.
He preferred sticking close to his cow.

During the day, the egret mostly rode on his cow's rump or perched on her shoulder. Often they talked. The cow had been places and seen things.

She knew about ukuleles and picnics.

She discussed kites and kayaks.

She had once tasted a toasted marshmallow.

The cow's stories gave the egret ideas.

At night, snuggled into the cow's neck,
he dreamed of reefs and beach umbrellas.

One sunny morning, the egret hopped onto the cow's head. "I might try flying."

"Do!" said the cow. "See the beach!
The sand squeaks like baby mice."

"I'd come right back." The egret still had the jitters.

"Absolutely," said the cow.

"And you'd be here the whole time." The egret felt a bit braver.

"Too true," said the cow.

The egret fluttered upward, hovering above the pasture. The view took his breath away! The ocean!

Down below, he saw the herd shuffling in a blurry circle.

"Back so soon?" The cow seemed surprised.

"I didn't go," said the egret.
"How would I ever find you again?"

"Obvious."
The cow twitched her ears.
"Watch for these."

Obvious!

A joyful surge hurtled the egret across the sky.
He scooped up a shell at the squeaky beach and then sped home.

Cows covered the pasture like an inky lake.
Every ear flicked and wiggled.

The egret zigzagged over the herd,
flapping back and forth.

WHERE'S my cow? WHERE'S MY COW?

At last he landed,
frantic and frazzled.

"I lost you!"

"How?" asked the cow.
"I've been wagging my ears like mad."

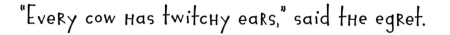

"Every cow has twitchy ears," said the egret.

The cow thought about it.
"Next time I'll switch my tail."

"Good plan." The egret pointed at the shell.
"Look what I found for you."

"Ooh," said the cow.

In the morning, the egret made a beeline
for the sea, skimming over the foamy surf.

He snagged a streamer from a kite caught in a palm tree
and then wheeled back, zooming over the dunes.

Cows drifted across the pasture like black clouds in a green sky.
Tails switched and hitched every which way.

Where's my cow? WHERE'S MY COW?

Finding her took ages.

"I thought you were gone!"
The egret felt wobbly
and weepy.

"I thought **you**
were gone,"
said the cow.
"I've been cracking
my tail like a whip."

"Every cow's tail is switchy," said the egret.
"Next time I'll shout, and you shout back."

The cow thought this was an excellent suggestion.

A breeze teased the streamer.
"Look what I found for you."

"Beautiful," said the cow.

The following day, the egret soared out to the marsh.
He stamped a pattern of tracks in the gooey mud and ate three shrimp.

He saw a sailboat.

He picked up a twisty stick.

The egret couldn't wait to tell the
cow about his adventure.

"Ma!
Ma!
Ma!"

he squawked.

Every cow lifted its velvety nose and mooed.

The egret flopped onto one wrong cow
and hopped across a dozen others before he found his.

"Finally." The cow's voice sounded scratchy.
"I shouted myself silly."

The egret wheezed. "Me, too.
Everyone on the ground is a cow, and everyone in the sky is a bird."

"Phooey." The cow frowned.
"We need something spottable from a ways away."

"Hey! Will this do?
  Look what I found for you."
      The egret stuck the stick in the ground.

"Something eye-catchy!
  Something upstanding!
      Something like . . ."

"...a flag!"

"Super!"
said the cow.

Now, every morning, the flock takes off
to explore the shore.

And at the end of the day, when the rosy sky
is full of birds and the pasture is full of cows,
the little egret wonders,

And **THERE** she is.

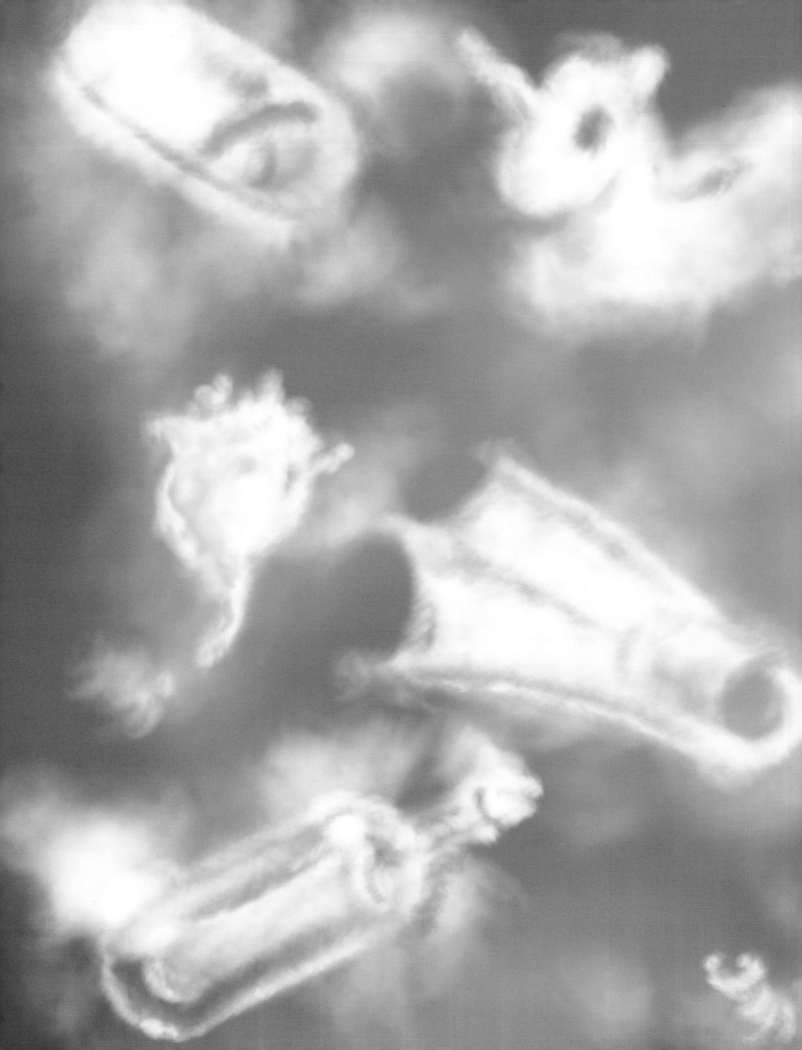